The Umbrella Queen

By Shirin Yim Bridges

Illustrations by Taeeun Yoo

Greenwillow Books

An Imprint of HarperCollins*Publishers*

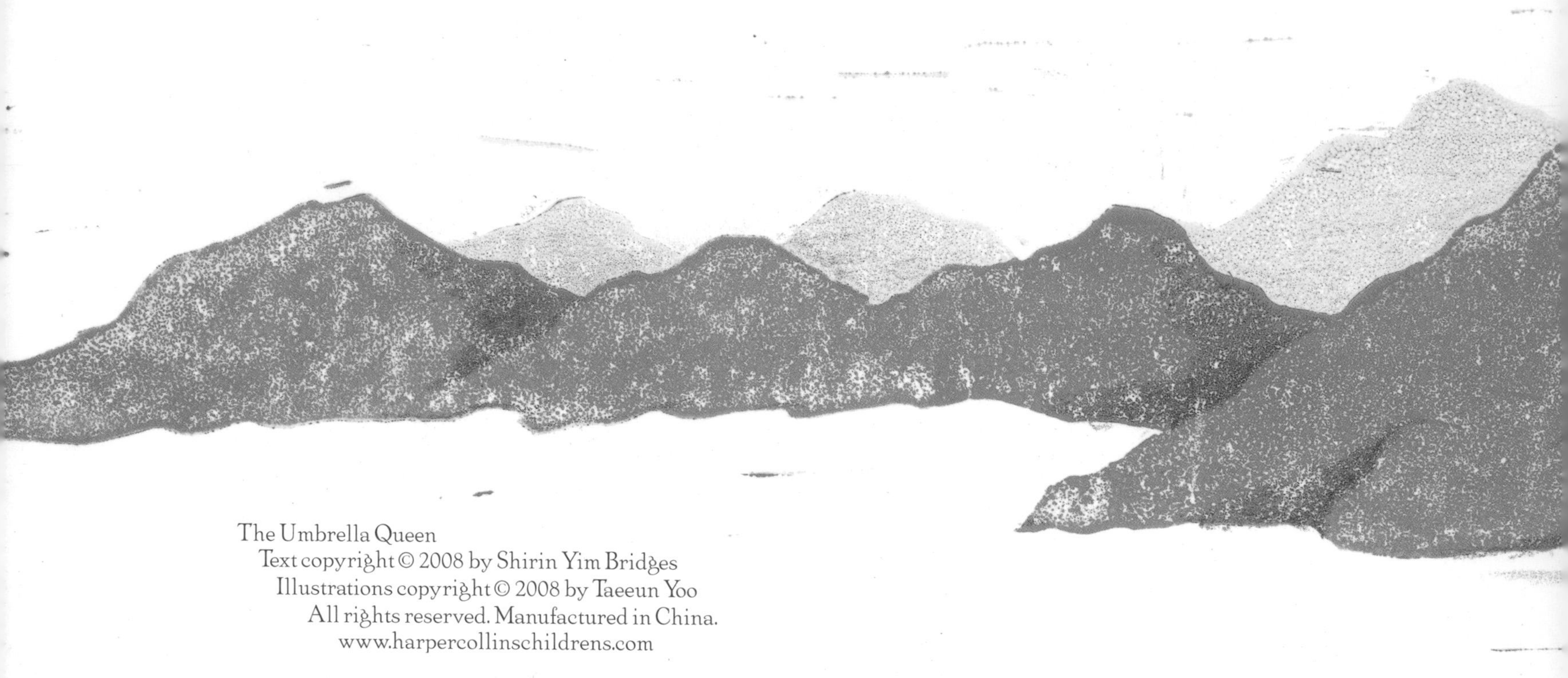

The Umbrella Queen

www.harpercollinschildrens.com

Linoleum prints with pencil were used to prepare the full-color art.
The text type is OPTI Artcraft.

Library of Congress Cataloging-in-Publication Data
Bridges, Shirin Yim.
The umbrella queen / by Shirin Yim Bridges; illustrations by Taeeun Yoo.
p. cm.
"Greenwillow Books."
Summary: In a village in Thailand where everyone makes umbrellas, young Noot dreams of painting the most beautiful one and leading the annual parade as Umbrella Queen, but her unconventional ideas displease her parents.
ISBN: 978-0-06-075040-4 (trade bdg.)
ISBN: 978-0-06-075041-1 (lib. bdg.)
[1. Individuality—Fiction. 2. Umbrellas—Fiction. 3. Painting—Fiction. 4. Thailand—Fiction.] I. Yoo, Taeeun, ill. II. Title.
PZ7.B75234Umb 2007 [E]—dc22 2005035730

First Edition 10 9 8 7 6 5 4 3 2 1

For Mom, who always read to us,
and for Dad, who always read *The Shy Bear*
—S.Y.B.

To my parents, with love
—T.Y.

High in the hills of Thailand, there is a village where everyone does the same thing, the same thing people in the village have been doing for hundreds of years: making umbrellas. Big umbrellas, small umbrellas. Paper umbrellas, silk umbrellas. Red, blue, yellow, pink, green umbrellas—all of them painted with flowers and butterflies by the women and girls of the village.

Every New Year's Day, the woman who has painted the most beautiful umbrella is chosen as the Umbrella Queen, and she leads all the villagers in a big umbrella parade. A little girl named Noot took part in these parades, walking behind older girls who were proudly carrying the umbrellas they'd painted. How Noot wished she had an umbrella of her own!

"When can I paint umbrellas?" she asked her mother.

Noot already knew how the umbrellas were made. She'd watched her father fit thin strips of wood and bamboo together to make the umbrella frames.

She'd helped her grandmother make paper to cover the umbrellas with. But what Noot wanted to do was what her mother did: she wanted to paint umbrellas.

“Please let me try painting. I promise I’ll be careful,” said Noot.

Noot’s mother was working in the garden. Freshly painted umbrellas were propped open around her like huge flowers. “Very well, Noot,” her mother said, giving Noot an umbrella. “Paint on your umbrella what I’m painting on mine.”

Noot's mother painted a flower. Noot painted a flower. Noot's mother painted some leaves and vines. Noot carefully painted leaves and vines. Noot's mother painted two butterflies fluttering around the flowers. Noot painted two butterflies fluttering around the flowers.

"That's very good, Noot," said her mother, impressed. "Let's show Phaw our umbrellas."

They put the two umbrellas in front of Noot's father. Noot's grandmother joined them. They all looked from one umbrella to the other.

"Why, you can hardly tell the difference!" Noot's grandmother said.

Noot's father gave his daughter a big hug. "With a little practice, Noot, you'll be a great umbrella painter!"

The next day, Noot's mother gave her five umbrellas that were ready to be painted. "Here's a finished one, Noot, so you'll remember what to paint," said her mother. Then her grandmother gave Noot her very own set of paints and brushes. Finally, her father helped her carry all her things to a spot she'd picked in the corner of the garden.

Noot sat in the sunshine and started to paint. First she painted the butterflies. Then she *was* going to paint the flowers, leaves, and vines. But something made her change her mind. She painted an elephant chasing the butterflies instead. Around the rim of the umbrella, the little elephant chased butterflies.

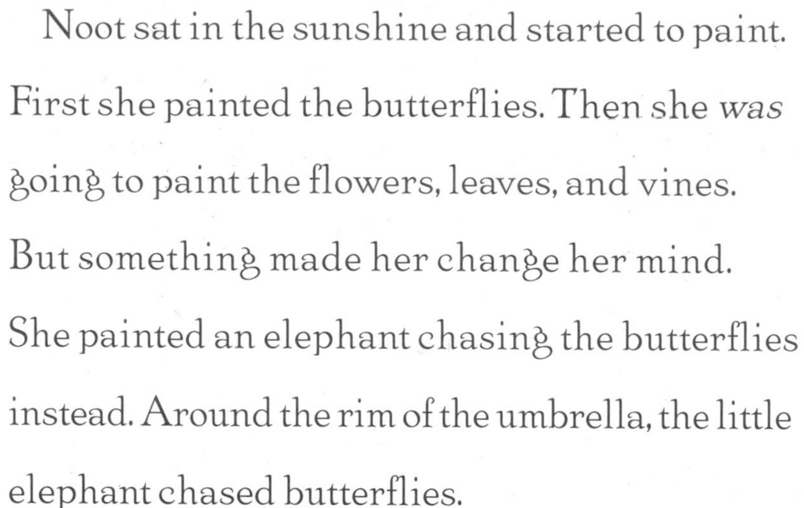

On her second umbrella, the butterflies had flown away. Instead, the little elephant, left alone, was practicing handstands. He did a handstand . . . and then fell down . . . and then got up and tried again.

On Noot's third umbrella, the little elephant was joined by another. The two elephants ran around and around, squirting each other with water through their trunks.

On the fourth umbrella, a whole string of elephants walked happily, trunk-to-tail.

And on the last umbrella, the elephants had fun just being silly.

"What are you doing?" asked Noot's mother, not very pleased. "You're supposed to be painting flowers and butterflies!"

Noot smiled. "But I like elephants," she said.

"I'm sorry, Noot," said her father. "You must paint flowers and butterflies."

"Yes, Phaw," said Noot, trying to hide her disappointment. She knew that all the umbrellas her family made were sold to the village council's shop, which sold nothing but flower-and-butterfly umbrellas. Painting umbrellas wasn't just for fun. It was work to help feed the family.

So every day for the rest of the year, Noot worked hard painting flowers and butterflies. But in the evenings, when the air rang with the laughter of children playing hide-and-seek in the street, Noot gathered up leftover scraps of bamboo and mulberry paper and made tiny, doll-sized umbrellas. And *these* umbrellas she painted with elephants and arranged proudly on her windowsill.

Before long, it was time to prepare for the New Year celebrations, including the umbrella parade. For the first time that anyone could remember, the King was going to be spending the New Year holiday in his winter palace nearby. The village council had taken the bold step of inviting the King to come to the village to choose this year's Umbrella Queen.

Every day, all day long, the women laughed and chatted while they worked in their gardens. They talked about whether the King would accept the invitation. Every evening, the men gathered under the big tree in the middle of the village and talked about the same thing.

Then, one morning two weeks before New Year's Day, the noise outside Noot's window woke her up. The whole village was shouting and laughing and calling out to one another. Noot scrambled out of bed to see what was going on. She could hardly believe it: the King had written to say he was coming to choose the Umbrella Queen!

On the big day, all the families gave their houses a final cleaning and laid their best umbrellas out by their gates, opened so that the painted flowers and butterflies faced the road. The King and the village councilors walked down the road, inspecting the umbrellas one by one.

Finally, the King stopped in front of Noot's house. He looked carefully at the umbrellas by the gate. "These are very beautiful umbrellas," he said to Noot's mother, who bowed deeply but kept her eyes respectfully cast down toward the ground.

The King looked down the road to make sure that this was the last house. All the villagers had now gathered a respectful distance behind him. Turning to them and smiling, he straightened his back to make his announcement. But as he did, something caught his eye. "What are those?" he asked, and stepped forward to take a closer look.

Noot's mother almost fainted to see the King peering through a window into her house.

"Who painted these strange umbrellas?" asked the King.

A murmur went through the crowd as they noticed the tiny umbrellas clustered along the windowsill.

"Look!" exclaimed the King. "They're covered with tiny little elephants!"

"Did you paint these umbrellas?" the King asked Noot, guessing from her red ears that she had.

"Yes, Your Majesty," replied Noot, bowing deeply.

"What is your name?"

"Noot, Your Majesty."

"Why such tiny umbrellas?"

"The big umbrellas are only for flowers and butterflies," replied Noot, keeping her eyes down.

"Hmmmm," said the King. "And what's wrong with flowers and butterflies? Why did you need to paint elephants?"

"Well . . . ," Noot stuttered, wondering how she could explain herself. She frowned and forgot to keep her eyes on the ground. She looked straight up and was surprised to see the King's friendly smile. "I like elephants."

The King laughed.

"Ladies and gentlemen," he said kindly, taking Noot's hand and turning around to address the rest of the village, "because she paints from her heart, I'm choosing Noot as this year's Umbrella Queen."